THE JOURNEY TO SPACE

THANVANTH S S

Copyright © Thanvanth S S
All Rights Reserved.

Contents

Preface

This book, The Journey to Space is a depiction of my own interest in the field of Writing books . This is my Second Book and the experience of creating a book is very useful.This book includes many Information and Facts and smooth flow of plot. It has interesting facts and mysteries for the readers to know more.

Book Description

This book describes a story of a girl in 2200. One day the girl found a Real diary, in that diary, many information and facts are shared by Mrs. Sarah. In the end, Mrs. Sarah shared some mysteries.
Who is Mrs. Sarah?
What is the Diary about?
What are the mysteries?

Read this story to unravel the mysteries in the diary.

Acknowledgements

This book guarentees the reader A new Information in every page. As an author, I never wish to hurt or pin-point any human or wrong doings. The characters and events of the story are completely imaginery and the information shared in this book also Scientificly Proved. I would like to thank every supporter of this small action, and look forward to more support from everyone.

Author Biography

I, Thanvanth SS, am a student who loves to express my thoughts and imagination to the society through my paintings and stories. " The Journey to Space " is my Second book, it is a Scientific Fiction . I am Very interested in art, craft and also other curricular and extra curricular activities. I look forward to more appreciation from the world outside.

CHAPTER ONE

A OLD DIARY

"It just happened . that on a beautiful day in the year 2200..... when anything and everything was different from now. There lived a family of 3 members - Jacob , his wife Josephine and their daughter Clara ."

It was the time of mechanical school, Clara was a bright student studying 6th grade, she loves to explore anything extraordinary.

She has a peculiar habit, which is to search the storeroom, because there she may find something new and something interesting.

The winter season started,
After finishing her homework, She thought to search the store room .

She found a real diary in the store room. She felt so weirdly because in her time there is only an online diary visible on computer screens.

She went to her mother and asked about the diary,
Her mother told,

Clara It is your Grandmother's favorite diary, do you know that she is an astronaut and she lived in the International Space Station.

Clara told , *Yes mom I know*

Josephine told , *Then you read the diary, you will be coming to know about some information and facts about space*
.

Clara Replied , *Sure mom I am going to read now .*

Josephine Said, *Then Enjoy*

Then Clara went to the balcony and sat in the chair and started to read the diary

"Let's see what is in Grandmother Mrs. Sarah's Diary , Lets Join with Clara ...."

CHAPTER TWO

MY EXPERIENCE

"Clara Turned the First page , Myself Mrs Sarah , My aim is to become an astronaut and explore the space and our galaxy , as I wished , an opportunity to go to the space came to me , I had shared my experience in this diary ."

One Day in My School, The school management took the students to a Planetarium for Educational purpose. there I saw the night sky using Telescope .

That time I Promised my Teacher that I will Become an Astronaut one day.

After My Graduation, I Joined a Space Agency , After working there I got an opportunity to go to space and work in the international space station.

Then my Training started,

On the First day it was quite difficult for me, but as days passed it become very easy for me .

A Telescope

Finally the day arrived ,
On 22 December , for the first time I entered into the space , the moment was indescribable, full of joy and happiness and a proud moment.

It was the unforgettable day in my life ....

CHAPTER THREE

OUR GALAXY

*"Clara **Turned the next page** , I am Passionate to learn about the space , I shared my own Information and Facts of the Space "*

Galaxy is a gravitationally bound system that consists of stars, stellar objects, black holes, and an unknown component of dark matter. There are more than 170 billion galaxies in the whole universe .

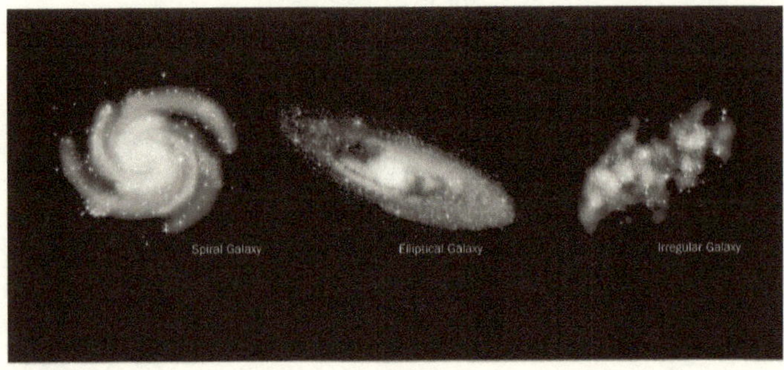

Galaxies may in the shape of spiral , elliptical or irregular .

There are thousands of planetary systems orbiting other stars in the Milky Way.

The planetary system is located in an outer spiral arm of the Milky Way galaxy is our Solar System.

OUR SOLAR SYSTEM

Our Planetary System is called "Solar System". The Word 'Solar' means things releted to Stars or Latin word of Sun "Solis". Our solar system formed about 4.5 billion years ago from a dense cloud of interstellar gas and dust. The order and arrangement of the planets and other bodies in our solar system is due to the way the solar system formed.

Our solar system extends much farther than the eight planets that orbit the Sun. Our solar system consists of our star, the Sun, andthe planets Mercury, Venus, Earth, Mars, Jupiter, Saturn, Uranus, and Neptune; dwarf planets such as Pluto; dozens of moons; and millions of asteroids, comets, and meteoroids.

THE SUN

Our Sun is a 4.5 billion-year-old star . It contains Hydrogen and Helium . Its gravity holds the solar system together.

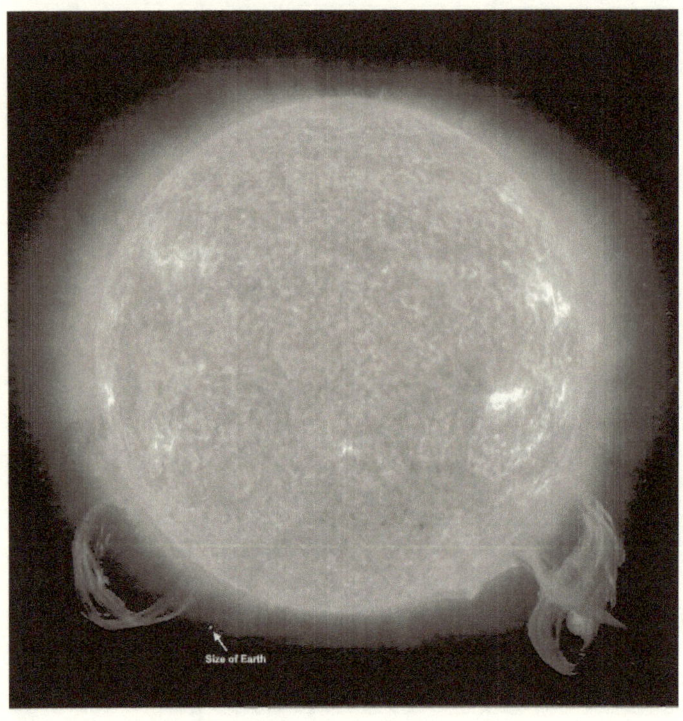

Core is the hottest part in sun - 27 million degrees Fahrenheit or 15 million degrees Celsius . Only Star in our Solar system .The Sun doesn't actually have a solid surface because it's a ball of plasma.

The Sun doesn't have any moons. It keeps our planet warm enough for living things to grow.

The Mercury

The smallest planet in our solar system. Nearest to the Sun. Mercury is not the hottest planet in our solar system.

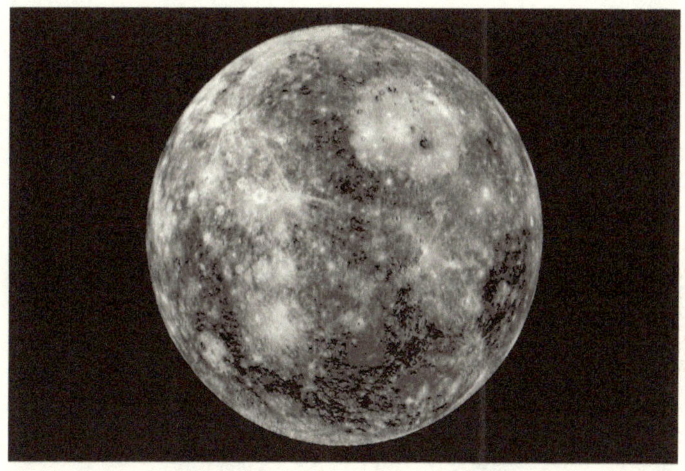

Mercury is elliptical – egg-shaped – orbit, and sluggish rotation.

Mercury is the fastest planet in our solar system. It is a Rocky Planet . It has No Moons and Rings .

The Venus

It is Earth's twin because it's similar in size and density.

It is the hottest planet in our solar system .

Venus has a thick, toxic atmosphere filled with carbon dioxide . Venus has crushing air pressure at its surface .

Venus is the only planet rotates on its axis backward. So the Sun rises in the west and sets in the east .

Venus orbits the Sun faster than Earth, however, so one year on Venus takes only about 225 Earth days .

The average surface of Venus is less than a billion years old.

Venus' thick atmosphere traps heat creating a runaway greenhouse effect .

Venus also known as Morning and Evening Star because it is visible in the sky at evening and is the last one to disappear from the sky at sunrise.

The Earth

Fifth largest planet in the solar system. Only world in our solar system with liquid water on the surface .
The name Earth is at least 1,000 years old.

Earth's atmosphere is 78 percent nitrogen, 21 percent oxygen and 1 percent other ingredients. It has One moon.

The Mars

Mars is also a dynamic planet . It has a dusty, cold, desert world with a very thin atmosphere.

Mars makes a complete orbit around the Sun in 687 Earth days.

Mars has two moons named Phobos and Deimos.
Mars is known as the Red Planet.

The Jupiter

The largest planet in the solar system. Jupiter is a gas giant . Eleven Earths could fit across Jupiter's equator.

Jupitar takes 12 Earth years to complete one orbit of the Sun.

Jupiter has more than 75 moons. Jupiter is a ringed planet .

THE JUPITER

The Saturn

It is a second-largest planet in our solar system .Saturn is a massive ball made mostly of hydrogen and helium.

THE SATURN

It takes 29 Earth years to orbit the sun.
Saturn has the most spectacular ring system. It have 7 Rings Combined.

The Uranus

Uranus is about four times wider than Earth. Uranus is an ice giant. It takes 84 Earth years to complete an orbit of the Sun. Uranus has 27 known moons.

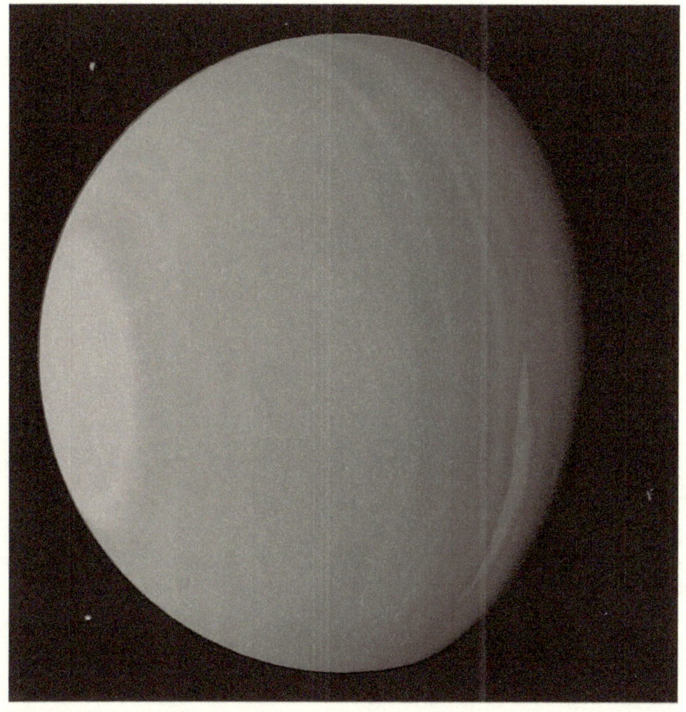

Uranus has 13 known rings. Like Venus, Uranus rotates east to west. But Uranus is unique in that it rotates on its side.

The Neptune

Neptune is the only planet in our solar system not visible to the naked eye. It takes about 165 Earth years to orbit the sun . Neptune's atmosphere is made up mostly of molecular hydrogen, atomic helium and methane. Neptune has 14 known moons .

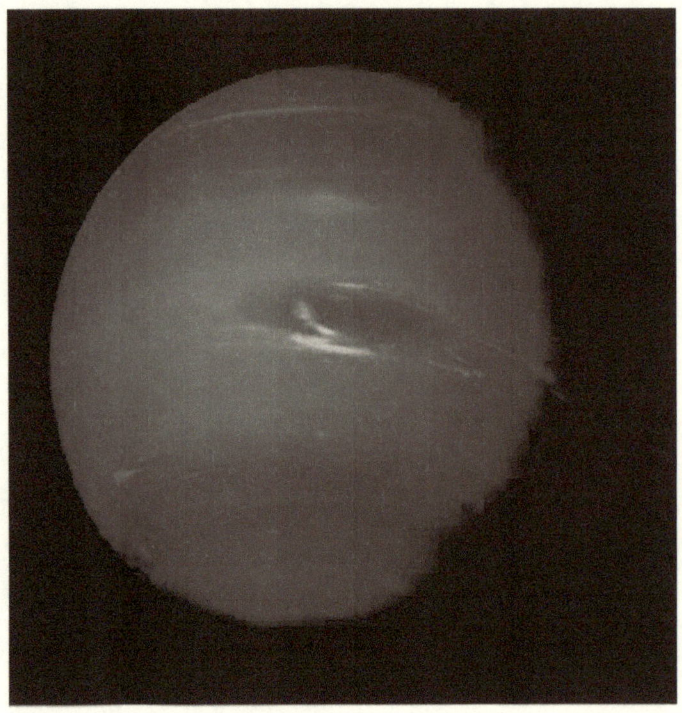

THE DWARF PLANETS

PLUTO : A year on Pluto is 248 Earth years. A day on Pluto lasts 153 hours, or about 6 Earth days. Pluto has 5 moons.

CERES : Ceres takes 1,682 Earth days, or 4.6 Earth years, to make one trip around the Sun. It doesn't have any moons

MAKEMAKE : Makemake has one provisional moon. Makemake takes 305 Earth years to make one trip around the Sun.

HAUMEA : Haumea takes 285 Earth years to make one trip around the Sun. it has Two known moons.

ERIS : Eris takes 557 Earth years to make one trip around the Sun. Eris has a very small moon called Dysnomia.

ASTEROIDS

Asteroids, sometimes called minor planets.

Most asteroids are irregularly shaped, though a few are nearly spherical.

METEOROIDS , METEORS & METEORITES

They're all related to the flashes of light called "shooting stars"

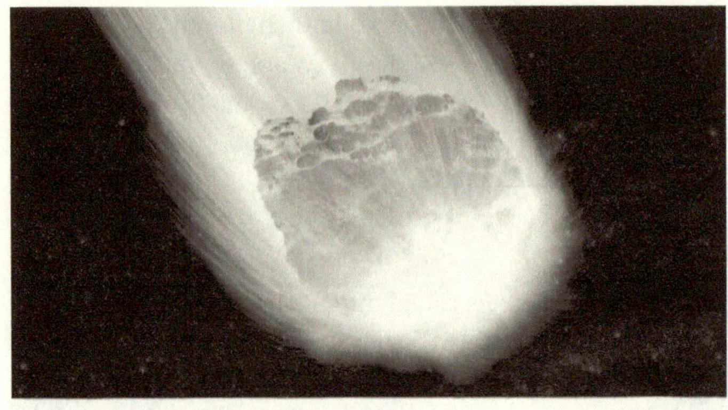

Meteoroids are objects in space that range in size from dust grains to small asteroids.

When meteoroids enter any planets atmosphere at high speed and burn up, the fireballs are called meteors.

When a meteoroid survives a trip through the atmosphere and hits the ground, it's called a meteorite.

COMETS

Comets are frozen leftovers from the formation of the solar system.

Comets are cosmic snowballs , Composed of dust, rock, and ices.

CHAPTER FOUR

INTERNATIONAL SPACE STATION

"Clara turned the next page , Still I worked in international space station , I very much excited to share some information about International Space Station"

The International Space Station is a large spacecraft in orbit around Earth.

The space station is also a unique science laboratory. Several nations worked together in space station.

It is Launched in 20 November 1998.

The space station has made it possible for people to have an ongoing presence in space.

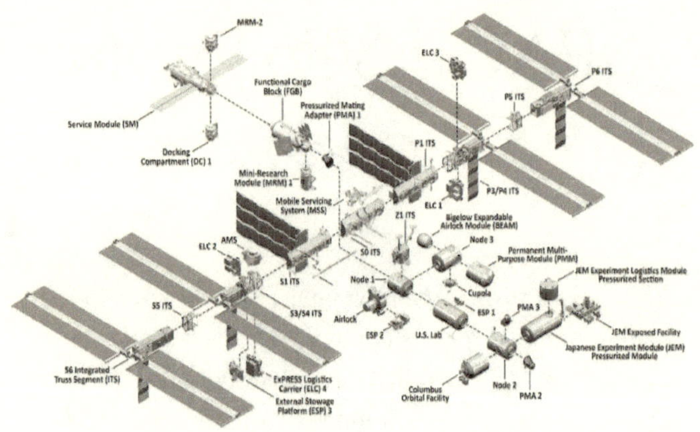

The space station has the volume of a five-bedroom house. is able to support a crew of six people. It is a Home to the Astrounats .

An international partnership of five space agencies from 15 countries operates the International Space Station.

In 24 hours, the space station makes 16 orbits of Earth, traveling through 16 sunrises and sunsets. This means it orbits Earth every 90 minutes.

CHAPTER FIVE

ROCKETS

"*Clara turned the next page* , Launching a rocket into space is one of humankind's crowning achivement.
"

Rocket is a vehicle that carries in object or a satellite or people to the space.

They come in different shapes and sizes but all rockets are propelled by engineers that produce thrust.

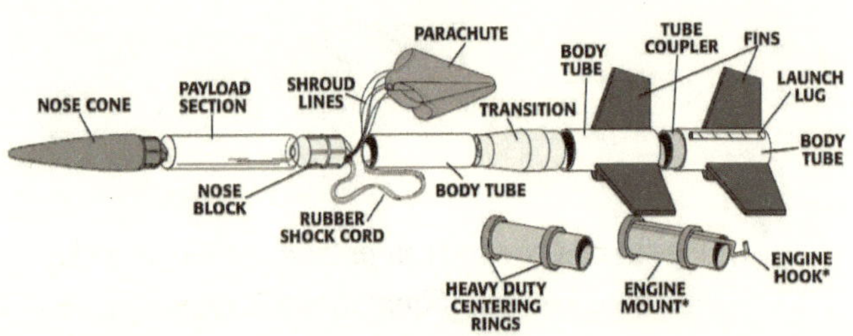

Rocket consist of a cylindrical body, nose cone and find.

90% of any rocket is fuel as the fuel gets consumed , the rocket keep disintegrating step by step.

At the correct altitude and speed , The upper stage engine cuts off completing the rockets journey from earth surface into orbit .

CHAPTER SIX

SATELLITES

> *"Clara turned the next page , The word "satellite"
> refers to a machine that is launched into space and
> moves around Earth or another body in space.
> "*

A satellite is a moon, planet or machine that orbits a planet or star. Earth is a satellite because it orbits the sun.

ARTIFICIAL SATELLITES

Satellites are used mainly for communications, such as beaming TV signals and phone calls around the world.

A group of more than 20 satellites make up the Global Positioning System or GPS .

With satellites, TV signals and phone calls are sent upward to a satellite.Then, instantly, the satellite can send them back down to different locations on Earth.

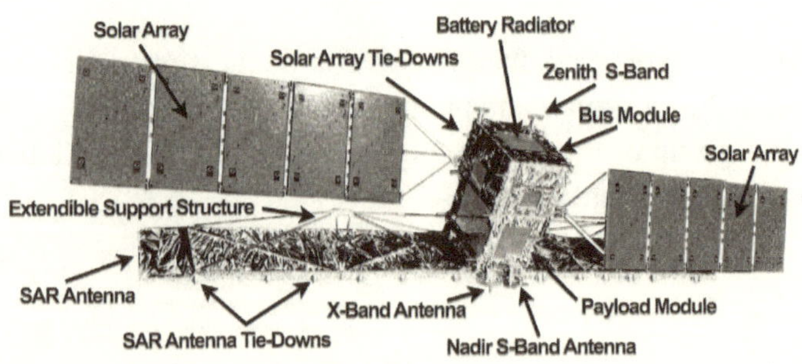

Satellites also can see into space better than telescopes at Earth's surface.

THE MOON - NATURAL SATELLITE

Moons – also known as natural satellites – orbit planets and asteroids in our solar system. Moons come in many shapes, sizes, and types.

Only Mercury and Venus Doesn't have Any moons.

- Mercury - 0

- Venus - 0
- Earth - 1
- Mars - 2
- Jupiter - 79 (53 confirmed, 26 provisional)
- Saturn - 82 (53 confirmed, 29 provisional)
- Uranus - 27
- Neptune - 14

CHAPTER SEVEN

MISSILES

> *"Clara turned the next page , Missiles are used during war , it is like a Weapon ."*

Missile is a guided airborne ranged weapon capable of self-propelled flight usually by a jet engine or rocket motor.

Missiles have five system components: targeting, guidance system, flight system, engine and warhead.

Missiles come in types adapted for different purposes:

1. Surface-to-Surface Missiles .
2. Air-to-Surface Missiles.

CHAPTER EIGHT

SPACE AGENCIES

"*Clara Turned the page* , *A Government of a country engaged in activities related to outer space and space exploration is called Space agency of an country.*"

NASA - The National Aeronautics and Space Administration

The National Aeronautics and Space Administration is America's civil space program and the global leader in space exploration.

NASA was Formed on July 29 1958 .

Headquartered in Washington, D.C. , United States

- *Neil Armstrong*

Neil A. Armstrong, the first man to walk on the moon, was born in Wapakoneta, Ohio,

On August 5, 1930. He began his NASA career in Ohio.

Neil Armstrong

International Moon Day was Celebrated annually on 20th of July , It celebrates the day Neil Armstrong first walked on the moon .

ISRO - Indian Space Research Organisation

• Origin of ISRO

The Government of India, formed the Indian National Committee for Space Research (INCOSPAR) under the leadership of Dr Sarabhai and Dr Ramanathan in 1962.

Dr Sarabhai

Dr Ramanathan

Later, the Indian Space Research Organisation (ISRO) was formed on August 15, 1969.

ISRO is the national space agency of India, headquartered in Bengaluru.

It operates under the Department of Space, Government of India. The prime objective of ISRO is to develop space technology and its application to various national needs.

- *Chandrayaan-1*

Chandrayaan-1, India's first mission to Moon, was launched successfully on October 22, 2008 from SDSC SHAR, Sriharikota.

The launch vehicle of Chandrayaan 1 is PSLV - C11

The spacecraft was orbiting around the Moon.

CHAPTER NINE

FACTS ABOUT OUR UNIVERSE

- Space is completely silent.
- The Sun is large enough that approximately 1.3 million Earths could fit inside.
- The Sunset on Mars appears Blue.
- The closest galaxy to the Milky Way is Andromeda.

Andromeda Galaxy

- The footprints on the moon will stay there for the next 100 million years.

- There is Floating water in Space.
- Every year the moon is drifting away from Earth by 3.8 cm.

CHAPTER TEN

UNSOLVED MYSTERIES

"Clara turned the last Page , It's no secret that space is full of mysteries. Here are some unsolved mysteries in space ."

1. Have Aliens ever visited earth?
2. What is inside the black holes?
3. Is That White hole the other end of the black hole?
4. What is Dark Matter In our universe?
5. Does our Universe has an end or it is a continuous one?
6. What is dark energy?
7. Is there any other planets in our Solar System ?

CHAPTER ELEVEN

THE PROMISE

*" Clara was finally finished reading the diary, and
she came to know that her grandmother's last wish
is to solve the mysteries "*

Clara went to her mother and told her,

Mom, I promise you, that one day I will Full fill my
grandmother's wish by solving mysteries in space.

Her mother told,

*Oh, my daughter, I am so proud of you, I hope that your will
full fill her wish.*

Definitions For New Words

"Here are some Definition for New Words Given in the Book ."

Mechanical school - Online School, Robotic Teachers

Peculiar - unusual or strange.

Astronaut - a person who travels in a spacecraft.

The international space station - Is a large spacecraft in orbit around Earth.

Planetarium - a building with a curved ceiling that represents the sky at night. It is used for showing the positions and movements of the planets and stars for education and entertainment.

Telescope - is an instrument in the shape of a tube with special pieces of glass (lenses) inside it. You look through it to make things that far away appear bigger and nearer.

Gravitational - the natural force that makes things fall to the ground when you drop them.

Stellar objects - relating to the stars or composed of the stars.

Thrust - to push somebody/something suddenly or violently.

Propel - to move, drive or push somebody/something forward or in a particular direction.

Satellite - an electronic device that is sent into space and moves around the earth or another planet for a particular purpose.

Disintegrating - to break into many small pieces.

9 798888 772385 3